ALSO BY ANNE RENWICK

ELEMENTAL WEB CHRONICLES

The Golden Spider

The Silver Skull

The Iron Fin

Venomous Secrets

ELEMENTAL WEB TALES

A Trace of Copper

In Pursuit of Dragons

A Reflection of Shadows

A Snowflake at Midnight

A Ghost in Amber

A Whisper of Bone

Flight of the Scarab

ELEMENTAL WEB STORIES

The Tin Rose

Kraken and Canals

Rust and Steam

Rust and Steam

An Elemental Web Story

Anne Renwick

To all steam train enthusiasts

ACKNOWLEDGMENTS

Sandra Sookoo, my wonderful editor who mercilessly ferrets out weaknesses and sets my work on a better course.

My husband and my two boys.

My mom and dad who instilled in me a love of both reading and travel.

Mr. Fox and his red pen.

CHAPTER ONE

The Great Northern Railway
Scotland, August 1884

"You proposed to Lady Delphinia?" His sister Clara gaped at him across a table covered with finely woven linen. Her fingers twitched and, for a moment, he thought she'd pitch her dinner roll at his forehead, but the bone china, glittering crystal and gleaming silver—all of it cast in a brilliant blue-white light from the Lucifer lamps affixed to the wood-paneled walls of the restaurant car—made her mind hard-won manners. Not to mention the upper-class passengers who shared the restaurant car as the steam train rattled and clacked its way at impressive speeds toward London while steambots rolled to and fro attending the gastronomical whims of the wealthy. "Why?"

Technically, he'd only spoken with the lady's father,

who was even now giving Mr. Benjamin Leighton's offer "all due consideration." Which meant the man was conflicted. Did he follow the traditions of generations? Or succumb to the temptations of allowing his daughter to marry a wealthy, upstart entrepreneur? Ben rather suspected Lady Delphinia's modest dowry would tip the decision in his favor.

"For the usual reasons." He refused to admit that the idea of binding himself to a woman with no chin bothered him. She was sweet and kind and the daughter of a gentleman. Certainly, there were other women interested in his wealth but, of late, Ben had lost all interest in the pursuit. The *ton* was correct. Better not to engage one's heart in the matter of marriage. "I require a wife."

"Of good breeding and societal standing." Clara's lips twisted as she parroted back words he'd spoken at the beginning of the London Season. "But Lady Delphinia is so very... very..."

Ben narrowed his eyes, warning her he'd not condone any disparaging comments.

"Meek," Clara settled on with a resigned sigh. "You truly mean to go through with this? You've no need of the *haut ton* and all their nonsense. Or a wife for that matter."

He lifted an eyebrow. His sister knew as well as he did that the fastest way into society's inner circles was through marriage. If he wanted to grow his business—

"We have enough. At least choose someone with a personality." Leaning on her elbows—with a glint in her eyes that told him her unrefined behavior was quite deliberate—

Clara lowered her voice. "Whatever happened? You spent the entire Season panting after Lady Alice Hemsworth and now the two of you occupy the same train carriage, frostily pretending that the other is not present."

Her words were a blast furnace. Heat shot through him, threatening imminent spontaneous combustion and welding every joint in place. He couldn't move. "She's here?" His voice—a scalded strangle—betrayed him.

"You didn't realize?" With a snort of laughter, his sister began to rise. "I'll just go—"

He slammed his foot down upon the hem of her skirts and growled, "Don't you dare."

Only Clara would dare to tweak his nose so. They'd grown up side by side, motherless and beneath the thumb of a man who couldn't be counted upon to bring home weekly wages. Food and coal were never a given. Tired of numb fingers and rumbling stomachs, they'd set out to provide for themselves. Clara had swept floors in a milliner's, quietly absorbing tricks of the trade, while Ben ran with the gypsy children on Clockwork Corridor, hunting for stray scraps of metal that their parents fashioned into mechanical art.

But those days were well behind them now. Lady Alice was one of the few who knew any details of his past. During a stroll in Hyde park, she'd confessed to an interest in clockwork mechanisms and asked how he'd built the Leighton Carriage Company—cornering the market on luxury steam carriages in London—and he'd cracked open his soul, confiding a few carefully concealed facts about his upbringing. As he'd spoken, she'd wrapped her arm about his and drawn him close.

He'd counted himself a lucky man to have found such a woman. Until she'd coldly cut him from her life.

"But—" Clara pressed.

"Don't." He spoke through gritted teeth.

Still, he found it impossible not to look. Shifting in his chair as a steam attendant ladled chilled cucumber soup into his bowl, he turned his head just enough to catch a glimpse of the woman who sat behind him on the other side of the restaurant car, alone. With her nose in a book.

His traitorous heart gave a great *whomp* behind his rib cage, then set a rapid pace, demanding more oxygen than his lungs could supply. As always, Alice took his breath away. Dressed in a pink confection of a gown, her blonde hair was crimped and twisted and tucked into inexpert loops by means of flower-studded hair pins. Several strands had already made their escape, trailing across her cheeks to tease the curves of her bare shoulders.

He snapped his head back—gaze forward—to glare at his sister. His *conniving* sister. Of all the trains... "How much effort was it, Clara, to arrange this coincidence?"

Laughter bubbled in her eyes. "Insignificant compared to the effort that will be necessary if I find myself a relation of Lady Delphinia." She lifted a finger when he started to object. "Don't try to convince me you've lost all interest in Lady Alice; even the roots of your hair have flushed." Her next words came on a whisper. "And both of you were conspicuously absent from the Lady Westmorland's ballroom for a full hour, only to return disheveled and gooey-eyed."

Denial stuck in his throat, and he nearly choked on the lie. "Nothing happened."

Everything had happened. The entire Season they'd courted. Flirted. Stolen kisses behind trees at garden parties. Held each other too close during waltzes. Whispered words of longing in alcoves of the theater. All of their ardor culminating the night of that ball when Alice had led him down a hallway and into a shadowy room, deftly turning the key in its lock.

She had been the one to push his coat from his shoulders, to unfasten the buttons of his waistcoat and shirtsleeves, to slip her deft fingers beneath his waistband and wrap them firmly about his erection. Half-dressed and mad with lust, they'd landed upon the chaise longue in a tangle. His face heated at the memory. She'd worn silk stockings. Garters. But *no* knickers. Urging him onward, Alice had buried her face in his neck and cried out his name. Aether, the mere memory of her unpracticed but determined seduction had him half-hard.

"Nothing," he repeated, staring down into the depths of his soup as if only there could he discover what had gone so very, very wrong. Some might say a young lady had lost her innocence, but he rather believed it was *his* that had been stolen. Along with his heart.

"Ha!" Like a pteryform with a sheep, Clara refused to drop the topic. "Which is why you left the house the next morning—top hat in hand—to speak with her father?"

And arrived at her family's townhome to find the steam butler waiting with a note on a silver salver.

I'm sorry. I cannot marry you. Please do not try to contact me.

The world had dropped out from beneath his feet. Even now, a month later, he had yet to find his footing. "Point taken. Now hush."

"Hush?" If anything, her voice grew louder. She kicked him in the shin and yanked her hem free from his foot. "You've been moping about for the past month. Fix it, Benny, before I'm forced to take further actions."

He knew that look. Clara had *plans*. "Lady Alice herself declined my suit, not her father." His words came through a clenched jaw. Though humiliation burned in his gut, only blunt honesty would nip any additional schemes in the bud.

"Declined?" Confusion clouded her face, then she frowned. "I'd thought better of her."

Yes, well, so had he. Hell, he'd gone and fallen in love. Instead, the knowing smirks of other gentleman informed him that he'd been nothing but a passing amusement. Her curiosity for the lower classes now satisfied, he was easily dismissed.

Save she'd never, not once, made him feel inferior. Could there be another reason she refused to see him? Had he been too hasty in turning his—lukewarm—attentions to another lady? No. She'd made her wishes quite clear.

He picked up the silver spoon and applied himself to the

tasteless soup, trying to push all thought of Alice from his head. In two hours' time, the meal would conclude and the train would stop in Newcastle, allowing him to return to his compartment, the better to pass another sleepless night. By morning, he would be in London where he would finalize negotiations with Lady Delphinia's father.

Around them swirled the refined conversation of the well-born, punctuated by the clinking of silver against fine china and the occasional guffaws of a portly gentleman who was much amused at his companion's animated recount of an event upon a recent airship voyage where passengers had been accosted by airship pirates. His friend vowed never to fly again.

Meanwhile, the back of his neck burned. Did Alice notice him sitting here, not ten feet away? Was she truly reading *The Chemistry of the Secondary Batteries of Planté and Faure*? Or merely staring at a blur of words, hoping that Ben would not cause a scene? Or had she already wiped him from her memory?

He drew his eyebrows together. So mired in his own misery, he'd not even thought to ask: why on earth was she—a young, eligible lady—on this train and dining alone, unchaperoned? Why was she in Edinburgh in the first place? Young ladies were to spend the summer months husband-hunting in London.

Not that the answer to either question was any of his business.

At the far end of the restaurant car, a door opened—letting in the rattle and clack and a rush of air—before slamming shut. All heads snapped up to see who would be fool enough to risk crossing through the gangway into the restaurant car while the train was at full speed. In a race to compete with the luxuries of airships, the Great Northern Railway had added first class sleeper compartments and restaurant cars, but passengers were strongly encouraged to move between carriages only when the train was fully stopped.

But Newcastle was over two hours away, and the man who stalked into the room—elbowing past a steam attendant and nearly upsetting a platter of grilled sole—was an impatient sort. Intent on his victim, Hugh Krause failed to notice Ben's presence or hear his soft curses.

As Ben's hand curled into a fist, his gaze locked with Clara's. She'd swatted away too many unwelcome advances of her own.

"Why, yes," she said, her face tight. "He has joined Lady Alice, and she looks none too pleased." The corner of her mouth hitched upward. "Tell me again how you have no feelings for her?"

But Krause wasn't known for harassing women; he had a reputation for stealing proprietary information of a technological nature. Alice must have something he wanted— which meant he'd grossly underestimated her interest in his work. *That* gave him pause.

Ben spun in his seat in time to watch the weasel yank the book from Alice's hands and snap it shut. Eyes narrowed and lips pursed, she leaned forward and hissed something that shoved an iron rod through Krause's spine. Not to be outdone, his reply—no doubt vile—drained every last drop of blood from her face.

Outraged, Alice leapt to her feet and—clutching an oversized reticule—marched past, retracing Krause's path, chin held high, ignoring all the gaping passengers. Pausing to snatch an open bottle of champagne from a bewildered steam attendant, she threw Ben a puzzled stare, then yanked open the gangway door and disappeared.

Krause leaned back in his seat, a smug smile plastered across his face and snapped his fingers to gain the steam attendant's attention.

Why had the German been allowed back on British soil? He'd been caught—red-handed—stealing trade secrets, repeatedly. Once in Ben's own factory, posing as an assembly line worker. His true employee and been found drugged and locked in a closet. Hause was a nasty piece of work and growing more ruthless as time went on.

Ben stood, but there was no damsel in distress to rescue. Krause made no effort to follow her. And Alice had made it clear she wished to have nothing more to do with Ben.

"Oh, for aether's sake," Clara said, holding out her dinner roll, still wrapped in its napkin. "An entire bottle of champagne on two spoonfuls of cucumber soup? Hurry," her voice mocked him, "save her from herself."

With a snort, he snatched the bread from her hands and followed Alice. Heartsick, he could only hope she wouldn't slam her door in his face.

CHAPTER TWO

What to do? What to do? What to do?

Allowing the porter to seat her in the restaurant car had been a mistake, but she'd been so very hungry. And so very certain she'd not been followed.

Alice spun about inside the compartment as the train rattled and clanked over the iron tracks. She glanced down at the neck of the bottle clutched in her hand. It wouldn't solve anything, but perhaps it would calm her racing mind? She took a long, unladylike swig, then set the champagne upon a table before dropping heavily onto a chair.

There was nothing *to* do, save lock herself away until the train reached London.

Toeing off her shoes, she let them fall to the soft carpet with dull thuds. A rather loud ticking sound caught her ear, and she caught up the watch pinned to her bodice. Was it malfunctioning? No, but its hands did inform her there were hours upon hours until she reached London. She tugged at the drawstring of her reticule and peered in the bag. Not from Watson either. He was still in "standby" mode.

The ticking stopped.

Good. She slumped backward and stared at her lap. Her last hope for a future alongside the Queen's agents, a zoetomatic, contained within an oversized, beaded reticule. There was no one to blame, save herself, if the Duke of Avesbury respectfully declined her proposal.

Should that come to pass, she might need to destroy Watson, rather than let the mechanical creature fall into the German's hands.

She'd been right to think that Herr Krause would refuse to let the matter drop, but she'd not been not fast enough on her feet. Despite all precautions, he'd followed her to Edinburgh and caught sight of her outside Professor Armstrong's university office. Tonight, Krause had finally caught up to her and confronted her publicly, hissing his demands across a table, all pretentions at negotiations gone. Had he known how close her invention lay, would he have snatched it from her hands?

When Alice had stormed out from the restaurant car—risking life and limb to escape the German—the thunderstruck look upon Lady Gatwick's face promised that by tomorrow the first whispers of Alice's name—now sullied by her solitary train journey—would reach society's ears. If this last-ditch effort failed, all of *ton* society's doors would be closed to her. Nothing, save her morning appointment—and perhaps not even that—could salvage her good name.

Presenting her invention to the Duke of Avesbury was of paramount importance.

A soft knocking sounded upon the door. "Lady Alice?"

Ben. *Aether.* It was too much to hope he'd followed her of his own volition. She'd seen Clara trying to catch her eye, but word of Ben's impending engagement to Lady Delphinia—a superficial twit—had reached Alice. His intended might not have much between her ears, but as the daughter of a baron with dwindling assets, she would be an easy acquisition. And—should he wish heirs—her hips were certainly wide enough.

Unkind of her to think such thoughts.

With a huff of frustration, Alice took another swig of champagne from the bottle. But it failed to douse the jealousy that burned like a lump of coal inside her chest. She had no right.

Ben had been clear from the beginning of their courtship that he sought a wife of good standing to grease his path into *ton* society. Under orders, Alice had played along, doing her best to learn everything she could of the successful entrepreneur, to discover any nefarious plots he might be hatching against the empire. Not only had she found nothing, but the deeper she dug, the more she'd grown to like Ben. The day he'd discussed with her—at length—about the necessity of correspondingly larger flow sections between successive rows of blading in steam turbines, she'd foolishly fallen in love with the man.

With a soft groan, she fell forward and, dropping elbows onto knees, stared down the throat of the champagne bottle.

Not now. Not here. Not after her reprehensible behavior at the ball. Her heart twisted and writhed behind her ribcage, begging her to open the door, to pull him into her compartment and pour out her woes. But she was sworn to silence. A societal liaison did not inform a target—not even one who had been declared a non-threat—that the Queen had once suspected him of treasonous behavior. Not even after being dishonorably dismissed from the service. Especially since her former employer—the Duchess of Avesbury—was married to the man Alice hoped would agree to become her future employer.

"I know you're in there, Alice."

Her face burned. She pressed the cool of the bottle's glass to her hot cheeks. What must Ben think of her? Such wanton behavior followed by a refusal to see him, no matter the many bouquets of flowers he'd sent or the notes attached professing his love and begging for an explanation. But their entire courtship had been based on a foundation of lies, and she could give him no answer. Not if she hoped to continue working for the Crown.

Reason had dictated she set him free, allow their paths to diverge so that he might find a woman without an agenda that could—at any time—run counter to his own. There was nothing to do, save continue along the course she'd set for herself.

"Open the door." His voice grew more forceful, and she could tell Ben wasn't going to walk away. He deserved better from her than a wall of silence. But of all the times for his gentlemanly honor to depart and more primitive instincts to assert themselves! Ought she be proud? Or resentful?

His absence from the restaurant car would be remarked upon, linked to her own sudden exit. She would be labeled a loose woman. But as she no longer required an unblemished reputation to snag an unsuspecting target and was instead embarking upon a career that would see her labeled an eccentric old maid, perhaps it no longer mattered?

A final guzzle of the bubbly wine sent a fizzy rush of false courage through her veins. She set the bottle aside, tucked her reticule into a corner of the compartment, and stood. If her steps wobbled a touch, it was the fault of the train that rocked upon its tracks.

The ticking of clockwork once again caught her ear. It seemed... closer. Was it all in her imagination, an effect of too much champagne on an empty stomach? It must be.

She cracked open the compartment's door and met Ben's dark gaze. Aether, how she'd missed him. His brown eyes seemed to crackle and spark as they stared down at her. A shame she must discourage their heat. "By morning, my reputation will run in the gutters like so much sludge, especially if Lady Gatwick decides to put it about that I passed the night entertaining a man in my compartment. You shouldn't be here. Not if you wish to secure Lady Delphinia's hand. Return to your soup and you might yet salvage your courtship." She hated each word that she forced from her mouth.

"Let me in," he all but growled. "I'm not leaving until

you tell me exactly how a man like Hugh Krause has made your acquaintance."

"Is your inquiry driven by professional or romantic jealousy?"

His eyes narrowed. "A topic that ought to be discussed privately. Let me in, or I will spend the night guarding your door."

"Guarding?" Tipping her head, she pretended to give the idea serious consideration, but already her heart was fluttering at the prospect of—

Of what? Another assignation? Yes, that was exactly what drove the heat rising inside her, despite the fact that Ben looked more inclined to snarl and snap rather than bestow one of his delightfully wicked kisses. But perhaps he might yet be convinced otherwise. Not that she was opposed to the idea of a few well-placed nips.

A slow, controlled intake of breath warned her that Ben was losing his patience.

Swinging the door open, she waved him inside. He wasted no time. With two long steps, he brushed past her, dropping a cloth-wrapped dinner roll beside her champagne bottle on the table. "With complements from my sister."

She fell back against the closed—and locked—door, mute. All she could do was stare—her mouth dry—and marvel at how his broad shoulders filled the confined space. There was barely enough room for both of them to stand within the compartment. With only a single chair, one of them would have to sit on the bed.

Bed.

An article of furniture they'd not had access to before. Though the chaise longue had served its purpose, she couldn't help but wonder what it might be like to disrobe at leisure, to explore Ben's form without fear of discovery, to curl against his side, basking in the glow of post-coital pleasure.

"Alice?" He tipped her chin upward with a single finger until her eyes met his. "All those questions about clockwork and steam engines were more than an intense interest in my business, weren't they?"

She couldn't deny it.

"I should have known." He drew in a deep breath. "Tell me what you've invented, and that you've not divulged the nature of your invention to one Hugh Krause. His business practices are beyond unscrupulous."

She sucked in a shocked breath that shattered her pleasant—if inappropriate—immodest thoughts. "You know him?"

"Unfortunately." Ben's lips pulled into a frown. "If you wish to sell your design—whatever it is—I'll double his offer."

Krause's offer *had* involved an obscene amount of money. But as a wealthy—if soon to be disgraced—heiress, the contraption she'd painstakingly designed and built was worth far more to her as a gift for the Duke of Avesbury. She'd always planned to complete her task as a societal liaison, then—once her husband was disposed of—pursue her true interest: engineering.

If her device met the duke's approval, if she could

persuade him to sponsor her application to the Rankine Institute, then perhaps her career might be accelerated rather than derailed. She longed to once again bask in the good graces of the Queen's agents.

To date, she'd never provided anyone—save the duke—with any details of her invention. How Herr Krause had caught word of it was a fact she'd been unable to discover. Then again, she'd not been discreet in the early phases of her work, while fiddling about with rough ideas for the various uses of clockwork and chemicals.

"It's not for sale," Alice said, twisting her face at the thought of Krause ever laying his sweaty, grasping hands on her zoetomatic. "He's just another man who doesn't know how to take 'no' for an answer."

Ben's face froze, and his hand dropped. "Understood." Eyes averted, he reached past her for the door handle, and she caught a whiff of spice and musk. "I won't bother you again."

"Not you." She pressed her palm to his firm chest. "I didn't mean *you*."

His lips flattened into a thin line. When he finally spoke, his voice was soft. "I thought we had something special. I wanted to marry you, even before our time together at the ball."

"We did." The lump in her throat threatened to choke off her words. For months, she'd looked forward to their wedding and had selfishly refused to disengage when the accusations against Ben were lifted. Stupid of her to think the Duchess of Avesbury would consider an accomplished

seduction a reason to allow Alice to marry. "It's just that...
It's complicated."

A loud ticking sound filled the compartment. *Could he
hear that?* She opened her mouth to ask, then snapped it
shut. No need to let him think she was insane.

"Complicated." His eyes burned. "I love you. You once
professed to return the sentiment. You enjoyed our activities, did you not?"

Her face was hot enough to set a match alight. "I did."
The understatement of the century. Her entire world had
shifted and rearranged itself that night.

His eyebrow quirked, waiting, no doubt, for her to utter
a reasonable explanation.

She took a deep breath. "I'm not who you think I am."
Eyes wide, she clapped a hand over her mouth.

Aether, even that much information was a reckless
admission.

CHAPTER THREE

He barked a laugh, tugging at his collar. "What are you, a spy?"

The enclosed carriage was unusually warm even for the month of August. Were they engaged—as they ought to be—he'd happily rid himself of his coat, tug on that pink ribbon at her back, and tumble them both onto the mattress behind him. A hasty coupling in the dark room of a manor house had only whetted his appetite, and he longed to explore—at leisure—a far larger expanse of bare skin than he'd managed to glimpse in the moonlight.

But the sharp intake of her breath and the bright flush upon her face took him by surprise, and he set aside his fantasy. Alarmed, her eyes darted about the compartment, unable to look directly at him, but unable to settle anywhere else.

A joke. His comment was a joke intended purely to lighten the situation. To imply something so utterly ridiculous that whatever secret she struggled to reveal would be easily pushed into the light.

A spy? Impossible. Alice wasn't one to dance about a topic, to mince words or dissemble. Then again, an unmarried, young lady of the *ton* didn't travel alone. Ever. As noted, by morning her reputation would be in tatters. He wasn't even in a position to assist her in its repair, for marrying him—a lower class upstart—would only shred it further.

If she would have him.

"Not exactly," she whispered.

Her eyes had finally settled, fixing upon the cravat tied about his neck, the very first item she'd removed the night she seduced him. Was she thinking of trying it again? Would he let her? He might. Most thought him a bloodthirsty business man but, in her hands, he was putty. And wasn't that just the point? Had a woman been sent to relieve him of trade secrets? *That* thought tightened his stomach.

Somewhere inside the compartment, a clock ticked—rather loudly—as if to suggest that their time together might well hinge on his next words. Then fell silent again. Odd, but irrelevant.

He struggled to recall the specifics of what he'd told her about his work. Nothing of any significant value that she could have passed to Krause. Yet here they were. Had Krause forced her somehow into a collusion, into a seduction? His stomach twisted. Had all that passed between them been lies?

A muscle jumped in his jaw.

"Not exactly," he repeated. "But you're not who I think you are?" Ben crossed his arms and stared down at Alice. He wasn't certain *what* to think. Upon reflection, perhaps their courtship had proceeded too swiftly, too smoothly. A romance that had not encountered a single rut the entire three months they'd known each other. Not until she'd cut him off with a terse note delivered to him by a steam butler. "Clearly. Unless you plan to offer an explanation, it would be best if you step away from the door and let me go." He frowned, reluctant to set an ultimatum, but enough was enough. "But I won't be back. I've no interest in foolish games."

"A moment." She brushed past him in a rustle of silk, ruffles and lace. Though he was momentarily distracted by the narrowness of the thin, pink ribbon that held the bodice of her dress closed, there was no mistaking her intent when she reached for the champagne.

He was faster.

She cried out, objecting as he snatched her crutch away.

"No." Holding the bottle behind his back, he shook his head slowly. "No false courage. Let's start with your name. Are you not Lady Alice Hemsworth?"

"I am." With a sigh, she sank down onto the chair. "I've told you no falsehoods, merely withheld... a part of myself." Lifting the dinner roll, she dropped it into her lap, picking at its crust and proceeding to eviscerate the hapless item.

A delaying tactic that spoke of nerves and reluctance.

Silent, he waited.

Staring at the bread crumbs, she cleared her throat. "I

was asked to gain your trust, to determine if you had any cause to take action against the British government."

"Me?" He snorted. Though he was often in negotiations with foreign business men and from time to time might grumble about politics, he had no cause—or desire—to betray his country. He had himself, after all, turned Krause over to the authorities. *Wait.* She worked for the Crown? "My loyalty was called into question? By whom? Why?"

"She never gave me details. Something to do with foreign business contacts." Alice lifted her gaze to his. "That's all I know."

"She."

"Please," Alice begged. "I'm sworn to silence."

Alice couldn't possibly be referring to the Queen, could she? He took a step back. "So it was all a ruse. You sacrificed your virginity on behalf of..." He lifted his eyebrows.

"It was no sacrifice." Her face flamed. "I was told to disengage. That you had been found not guilty. I learned I was to be presented with a new name—a new target—the following day. But I didn't want to move on. I thought, perhaps, if we'd... if I'd been compromised..."

Picking his jaw up off the floor, he finished her thought. "That you could, what, keep me?"

"Something like that."

"You planned to marry me—a mere commoner—then carry on with your activities?" As he spoke, his voice rose until he was all but shouting. "Seducing other men behind my back at the Queen's command?"

"No! Never! I would never behave in such a manner."

Her voice matched his own outrage, and she tossed aside the ruined bread, jumping to her feet. Crumbs fell to the floor. "I'd fallen in love with you. But, yes, I did—do—hope to still be of use to my Queen and country."

He gaped as pieces of his world came unglued and dropped to the ground with the crumbs. Ben struggled to imagine where—how—they now fit into his life. If at all. "How?"

Alice dragged in a deep breath. "A *married* societal liaison is, upon occasion, permitted to advance her career by training with and serving as a member of the Queen's agents."

Queen's agents. He'd heard the speculation about a select group of men trained in all manner of scientific fields —biological, chemical, mechanical, and so on—who were employed to keep the nation safe from unwanted interference in such technologies. Alice was one of them?

"As a wife—and eventually a mother—I would have, of course, kept close to home." She squirmed on her chair. "But such a path is closed to me now. The day after our... encounter, I was dishonorably dismissed for my actions. I've but one chance to resume my career. I've an audience with a high-ranking individual who might be convinced to sponsor my enrollment at the Rankine Institute."

"The engineering school?" His eyebrows drew together. "Insofar as I am aware, female applicants are unwelcome."

"Unwelcome, perhaps. But I've learned that one woman has completed a course of study and graduated with honors."

"And you intend to be the second."

Alice drew herself up straight. "I do."

He stared at her, his gut churning with regret. Not because she wished to pursue an engineering degree, but because she had not thought to confide in him that she harbored such a dream. He had to ask. "Why—as you profess to have fallen in love with me—did you turn me away?" He held up a hand when she opened her mouth to protest. "Did you think so little of me, that you thought I would prevent you from pursuing your own dreams?"

"You courted me for my social status, for my ability to introduce you to members of the *ton*, not for my clockwork skills." She glanced away. "Besides, how could you ever forgive me for so great a betrayal? For happily flirting as I led you by your cravat toward a prison sentence?"

Again her eyes fell upon his throat. The corner of his mouth quirked upward. She still wanted him. "I will admit to being rather miffed at your lack of trust, moreso at your willingness to let me court Lady Delphinia without protest."

She pursed her lips and narrowed her eyes. "You were rather quick to perch in her parlor."

"Perch?" He rolled his eyes. "I don't perch, and I'm *not* a traitor. And I've no objection to your designs upon pursuing an engineering degree or to your desire to work for the Queen's agents." Rather than despising the idea, he rather admired it. It took nerves of steel to buck the status quo and strike out on one's own. The two of them would make a fine pair, refusing to knuckle under to the demands society tried to place upon them.

"You don't?"

"None." He took a step closer, letting the wool of his trousers brush against the silk of her skirts. They stood mere inches apart now. The pulse at her neck jumped, a very satisfying response, for his own heart now thumped harder. Was he truly ready to throw aside every plan he'd made for Lady Delphinia? Indeed, he was. "Would marriage to me still be an impediment to your plans?"

"Not exactly." Her words came out on a breath of champagne-sweetened air. Her fingers wrapped about his cravat, pulling him closer still. "Am I forgiven for my error in judgment?"

"Mostly." He let his hands fall upon her waist. Dipping his head, he brushed his lips softly across hers. A final chance for her to push him away.

Instead, she parted her lips and gave a tug, moaning as he deepened their kiss. He yanked her hips against him, letting her feel how much he still desired her. Arms twining now about his neck, she crushed her soft breasts against his chest and slipped her tongue into his mouth to tangle with his own. He tasted champagne. Could one grow drunk on a kiss? For he certainly felt unbalanced. Reasoned thought evaporated with the steam that welled between them where their bodies touched, and he found his hands—as if of their own accord—bunching the fabric of her gown at her hips as blood rushed through his veins.

The train rattled and clanked over a stretch of poorly laid rail, throwing them off balance and against the wall. The jarring movement had restarted the ticking he'd heard earlier. Her project? Recalled to reason, he loosed his hands and let her skirts fall. Carnal activities needed to wait.

He brushed his thumb over the soft pink of her cheek. "Forgiven. Now, tell me what it is Krause so desperately pursues. I must have something to do with your mechanical inclinations." An informed summation. Krause would have no interest—well, no hope—in courting such a high-born woman as Lady Alice.

Ben himself had—to hear the gossips—far overstepped his place. An entrepreneur reaching for a societal rung too far above his head. They'd be right. He'd wanted to wed the daughter of a peer. Before today, he'd hoped for nothing more than an entrée to inner circles, convincing himself he could be content with the likes of Lady Delphinia. Except it was clear Lady Alice had stolen his heart.

And the notion that he would be wed to a spy was more an aphrodisiac than a deterrent.

"It's hours upon hours until we reach London," she said. "Can we talk about him later, perhaps while lying down, after... testing the bed?"

He laughed. "Tempting as that offer is, I wish to see this marvel you've constructed first." It was the only way to determine if Krause presented a true threat. The man was unscrupulous, and pains might have to be taken to discourage him.

"Very well." With a frown that spoke of regret, Alice trailed her fingers over the buttons of his waistcoat, then turned to retrieve her oversized reticule. Sitting once more upon the chair, she drew it onto her lap. "It would be easier simply to show you." Her nimble fingers unknotted the drawstring, much like they'd once deftly relieved him of his cravat.

Shrugging off his coat and tossing it aside, Ben dropped onto the edge of the bed. A necessary maneuver to conceal his body's rampant interest in anything *but* her device. *Soon.* The moment he had a comprehensive grasp of her skills—and Krause's motivations—he would draw her once more into his arms, picking up where they'd left off. He expected the rocking motion of the train would lend itself nicely to mattress exercises. And—were she favorably inclined—they might explore a few standing positions as well.

Loosening his cravat, he forced himself to focus upon the object she cradled in her hands. It was a round, silver sphere comprised of several curved, articulated segments. He lifted his eyebrows, wondering at what was concealed within. "It unfolds?"

"It does." She handed him the ball, then pointed. "That small prong? Give it a twitch, then run your hand over its surface."

He followed instructions and gave a low whistle when a metal creature uncurled and leapt onto four silver feet. Metal spines—spikes—jutted from the many perforations in its surface. Two green eyes that glowed from within blinked up at him, as if awaiting instruction.

"Meet Watson." Pride danced in her eyes. "My zoetomatic hedgehog."

"You built this yourself?" Of course she had. She concealed an impressive talent beneath the façade of a proper, young lady. The corners of his mouth lifted and an unusual warmth spread through his chest. No, not so proper. Alice was a woman he'd be proud to call his wife. If he could only convince her...

"I did."

"The craftsmanship is equal to—or perhaps even exceeds—the work of many talented Roma of my acquaintance." The highest compliment he could give her work. But like her, he suspected the contraption hid much beneath its charming surface. "Will you show me its many features? Or is that to be reserved only for the eyes of the Queen's agents?"

Alice chewed on her lip, a certain sign that the creature possessed hidden attributes. A moment of truth. How much did she trust him?

CHAPTER FOUR

Her heart hopped and skipped inside her chest, then all but skidded to a halt. She'd underestimated Ben. Instead of disgust, his eyes gleamed with pride. If anything, her admission that she had worked for—and intended to pursue a career with—the Queen's agents had piqued his interest. Her presentation of the zoetomatic had sealed it.

There was only one way to find out. Drawing in a deep breath, she opened her mouth.

But the loud ticking had started again. Ben's gaze dropped to the floor.

"Don't move." The sudden ice in his voice froze her to the core as he set Watson aside and knelt upon the floor. "There's some kind of beetle crawling up the hem of your skirt."

An insect? A shudder ran across her skin as she fought to hold still while the train rattled and rocked. Beetles were horrid things with too many legs that allowed them to move entirely too fast. Kicking would only entangle the tulle netting of her skirt or, worse, startle the creeping creature into skittering across her gown faster in a mad dash to take cover.

"Get it off!" she gasped, a desperate plea. If it dove behind her bodice, she *would* scream.

What was taking so long?

She made the mistake of allowing her gaze to drop. Ben knelt at her feet. In one hand he held a shoe, while he reached with his other hand for an overlarge beetle that glinted a dull copper. A long, slender proboscis extended from its head. This was no ordinary beetle.

"It's mechanical," Ben said, his voice entirely too calm. "And no doubt malevolent. I've heard rumors about Krause and the nasty little clockwork creatures he's thought to possess."

What was this creature about? "Watson. Assess." A few feet away, the zoetomatic's spines retracted, then were replaced by the environmental probes.

The train bumped over a poorly laid section of track, and the clockwork beetle dove into a fold of her skirts. Ben cursed under his breath.

"Poisonous?" she squeaked. She wrapped her shaking hand around the neck of the champagne bottle, ready to smash the beetle to smithereens should the opportunity arise.

"Most likely." Ever so carefully, he pulled at the tulle and silk of her skirt, searching. "There it is." His hand darted forward and, catching the beetle between thumb and forefinger, he attempted to pluck it from her gown—but its barbed legs had caught upon the tulle. "A moment longer." He dropped the shoe, then set about freeing the insect from the delicate netting, before holding it aloft, triumphant.

Watson began to ding an insistent alarm, confirming their worries. The insect did indeed harbor a dangerous chemical. She pressed her lips together. Though the zoetomatic's response time needed improvement.

"That does it," Alice muttered. "This is a declaration of war." She loosed a few choice curses, all of them directed at one Hugh Krause.

Ben's laughter rumbled, sending a thrill buzzing across her skin, reminding her how very much she wanted his touch to follow. She turned, setting aside the bottle to dig into her valise, hunting for a container large enough to imprison the clockwork beetle.

"Watson. Desist." Her order quieted the hedgehog, returning him to standby status.

A hiss of pain met her ears, and she glanced over her shoulder to find a grimace upon Ben's face.

"Hurry," he urged her. "The bastard installed a second needle with retrograde action. From the rapidly spreading numbness in my fingers, I'm not going to be able to hang on to this contraption much longer."

Aether. She yanked her container of face cream from her valise and unscrewed its lid. "Shove it in this. The oils should gum up the mechanisms enough to immobilize it."

And wouldn't destroy the beetle. They could study it later. Use it as evidence.

With clumsy fingers, Ben pushed the critter into the thick white ointment, and she slapped the lid back in place, screwing it tightly closed. She shoved the entire container into her reticule. This was something the duke ought to know about. He himself had commissioned the construction of Watson—based on the blueprints she'd presented—and would wish to know that a man such as Krause presented a decided threat.

"I think... perhaps I'll stay on the floor for the time being." Ben's face was too pale.

Another woman might run for help, but—though panic tightened her throat—Alice had taken note of every single passenger. Not one physician numbered among them. There was no assistance to be had. Bursting into the restaurant car and yelling for help would only cause a kerfuffle. She needed to stay calm, to carefully assess Ben's condition.

"How bad is it?" She dropped to the floor beside him, lifting his hand and frowning at the droplet of blood that welled upon the pad of his thumb. Though the beetle had not touched her skin, tiny ice-cold feet skittered down her spine. Poison. But what kind? Societal liaisons were taught to recognize the symptoms of only the most basic of poisons, but their training in that arena was sadly lacking. Which was why—while working on Watson's chemical analysis systems—she'd borrowed a certain book from Mr. Black, insisting that ballrooms could be just as dangerous as was any form of fieldwork. With grudging reluctance, he'd leant her the text for a few precious nights, warning her that the owner—Miss Cait McCullough, from the name inscribed in its cover—expected it back soon. Curiosity burned, but she'd been too intimidated by him to ask who Miss McCullough was. She'd burned the midnight oil, devouring its words and taking copious notes, but could she now recall them? Panic nipped at her calm. "Tell me what you're feeling."

"The numbness is spreading rapidly," he said. "It's reached my elbow."

"Any internal sensations?" She placed a palm against his forehead. A touch clammy, as would expected by mild shock. Fingertips touched to the inside of his wrist told her his pulse was only slightly elevated. "Lightness of breath? Change in heart rate?"

He shook his head. "None." A smile curved his lips. "But press your face to my chest, my lady, to be certain."

With a huff of exasperation at his flippancy, her mind paged through Miss McCullough's book of poisons, alighting on a few possibilities, few of them good. Ice crystalized in her veins. "If the toxin is crinlozyme, then—"

A knock sounded at the door. "Lady Alice?"

Her eyes caught Ben's. "Herr Krause," she whispered.

"Don't answer," he said, his voice hushed. He pushed himself onto his knees and dragged his discarded coat close. "If he thinks you've succumbed to the poison, he'll try to enter, and we'll have him caught, red-handed."

"Caught?" Alarm crept into her whisper. "You want to take him prisoner?" She had no weapons, no skill at hand-to-hand combat, and Ben's right arm now hung limply from his shoulder.

"It stands to reason that a man prepared to employ such a toxin would carry the antidote upon his person."

Ah. They *needed* to take him prisoner. The coiled tension in her gut unwound by the slightest degree. She could do this. They *had* the advantage. Two against one. And their attacker no doubt expected her to have succumbed to his assault beetle. He would enter unprepared for resistance.

"Lady Alice, I'm afraid we must speak." Herr Krause's words might be polite ones, but that was for the benefit of anyone in adjacent compartments who might overhear him. Given the harsh words he'd spat at her across the dining table and the clockwork beetle he'd sent to subdue—kill?— her, he wasn't about to let the matter drop.

"Best to take him alive, but..." Ben slid his left hand into his coat and withdrew a pistol. With a click, he cocked the gun and pushed it into her hand. "You have two shots. Don't fire unless you must, and please don't shoot at all if I'm in the way."

"What are you going to do?" Anxiety edged her voice. But she tamped it down and took the heavy weight of the weapon into her shaking hand. Aim. Pull the trigger. How hard could it be? *Very.* Difficult enough that Mr. Black had refused her lessons. *This* was a bad idea.

A furtive metallic scratching caught her ear. Herr Krause was picking the lock!

At their feet, Watson began to ding softly.

"Trip him. Punch him. Whatever I can manage." Ben picked up the ringing zoetomatic and regarded him with interest. "You programmed Watson to sound an imminent breach alarm?"

"I did." Despite the threat, pride still swelled in her voice.

"I don't suppose he has any useful attack features?"

"I'm afraid not." She made a mental note to add one, praying that there would be such an opportunity. "Watson. Quiet." The dinging ceased.

"A shame." He tucked the hedgehog beneath the bed, then struggled to gain his feet. Half-falling against the far wall, he waited. "We subdue Krause, then—as I don't know how much longer I'm going to have use of my limbs—you'll search his person for the antidote. A vial of liquid matched with a syringe. Perhaps a packet of powder."

Her hand tightened on the pistol. "Then force him to tell me how to administer the cure."

Click. The lock upon her door popped free.

"If he resists, don't hesitate to take your best guess." Ben's right eye twitched and his lungs heaved as he struggled to raise his left arm above his head. "I'd very much like to continue our early discussion. About a future. Together."

The door swung open, and Ben flung himself onto Herr Krause's back, wrapping his arm about the man's throat in an attempt to cut off his airflow. They fell to the floor in a tussle, locked against each other inside the small, confined space.

Alice lifted the pistol, hoping for an opportunity to shoot

Herr Krause in the foot. The leg. The arm. Someplace not too vital. Later, she would want answers.

Red-faced, Herr Krause clawed at Ben's arm, kicked at his shin, and jammed elbows into his stomach. Through it all, Ben never released his hold, though she could see him weakening as the poison flooded his system. At full strength, he would already have emerged the victor.

She *had* to do something!

Pointing the barrel of the weapon at the German's leg, she pulled the trigger. *Bang!* But this was the first time she'd ever fired a weapon. And she'd flinched and missed. *Dammit.*

She had, however, drawn the man's attention.

Herr Krause's leg swung in her direction, sweeping her feet from beneath her. With a cry she crashed to the floor in a heap of petticoats and ruffles. Worse, the pistol slid across the floor and beneath the bed. Not that it was any use in her hands. Better to hit the horrible man over the head with something.

Heart in her throat, she frantically searched the compartment.

Ben's shoe?

No, the champagne! Staggering to her feet she lunged toward the table, grabbing the bottle by the neck and hefting it into the air. With a single step she loomed over them. Ben caught her eye, gave her a nod, then rolled—pushing Herr Krause onto his side and laying his head at her feet. With a cascade of frothing wine, she brought the base of the bottle down upon the side of man's head.

He fell limp.

But for how long?

She dropped onto her knees, landing in the foaming puddle, and began to search Herr Krause's coat with shaking hands. A pocket watch. Lock picks. A handful of coins. A key. A pen knife. Papers. But no vials, no packets. She thought the drug might be crinlozyme—a paralytic that did not stop the heart or the lungs, but merely paralyzed its victim, leaving them helpless and conscious for up to twenty-three hours.

But Herr Krause—predatory industrialist thief—ought not have access to such a substance. And that was cause for extreme concern. He'd been seen conversing with her in the restaurant car, but the man had no scruples. He might *prefer* not to be linked to the death of a young lady, but he was a German citizen and could easily abscond with her Markoid battery to distant shores without fear of repercussions.

And that—combined with Ben's lethargic movements, shallow breaths and pale skin—had her worried. No, not worried. She was sliding down the razor's edge of fear. If it wasn't crinlozyme, it was likely deadly. Whatever the toxin, it had been calculated for her weight—a good two to three stones less than Ben. The only reason he'd managed to put up any kind of fight at all. And time was running out.

Panic wouldn't help. Alice closed her eyes, forced herself to draw in a long, deep breath. Pockets were too obvious. Items too easily lost from them. A prepared assassin would keep the antidote in a secure location. And concealed. Perhaps it was sewn into the very fabric of a garment?

Her eyes snapped open, and she grabbed fistfuls of Herr Krause's coat, using her hands to hunt for inconsistencies. Nothing. Closer to the chest? She searched his waistcoat. There. A rectangular patch. With the man's own pen knife, she slashed through the fabric. Tacked to the fabric with a few loose stitches was a packet of powder.

"I have it!" she cried, lifting her gaze to Ben's. "But it's unlabeled!" What had she expected? A detailed protocol? Given she'd not found a syringe, the antidote was probably meant to be dissolved in water. All she had were the few tablespoons of champagne that remained in the bottle. But— "What if it's not the remedy, but something worse?"

"Try," Ben gasped, all but immobile. "Please."

Not at all encouraged that he now fought to draw breath, Alice planted a knee upon Herr Krause's chest as she climbed across the villain to reach Ben. Ever so carefully, she emptied the white powder—every last ounce—into his mouth. Mucous membrane absorption was a start, but what if he needed to swallow it?

She tipped the edge of the champagne bottle to his lips, dribbling the remaining liquid into his mouth. Ben struggled to swallow.

Only then did Alice notice more than her hands were shaking. That beneath her knees, Herr Krause stirred.

"Tie," Ben breathed, his words still slurred. "Hands. Feet."

Yes, of course. But first—to be on the safe side—she

walloped the German once more with the champagne bottle.

With trembling fingers, she untied Ben's cravat and slid it free. Dragging Herr Krause's hands behind his back, she tied them together, yanking the knot tight. She pulled the man's own cravat from his neck and repeated the procedure at his ankles.

Heaving and shoving at the horrid man, Alice managed to push him aside so that she could kneel beside Ben, draw his head into her lap, and brush her trembling fingers through his thick hair. Her heart pounded. Her stomach hurt. And every breath was an effort. Any moment, the antidote—if, in fact, it was one—ought to take effect. She kept the champagne bottle close, just in case Herr Krause again became a problem.

"Any better?" He had to be. Her mistake to have turned away the one man she loved, a man who—as it turned out—would not only support but encourage her interests. Would he still wish to marry her, now that he'd had a small taste of the dangers that might pursue her?

Beneath her, the train rattled and shook, speeding toward London. Its other passengers oblivious to the drama unfolding a carriage away. She brushed her hand over Ben's face, over the rough stubble that edged his jaw, all while watching the rise and fall of his chest. It was steadier now.

"Ben?"

His arm lifted, and he caught her hand in his. "Better." He pressed a soft kiss to her palm.

Tears of relief welled in her eyes. She brushed them

away. "Thank aether, for a few minutes..." No, she'd not finish that thought aloud.

Ben rolled onto his knees and pushed into a seated position before wrapping an arm about her to draw her close. "If you're intent upon pursuing this," he glanced at the seemingly unconscious German and chose his word carefully, "career of yours, perhaps you won't object to a proposal over a prone body."

"Of marriage?" Her heart began to race again, this time with anticipation. "Are you certain?" Her eyes flicked to Herr Krause. "I don't anticipate this becoming a regular occurrence, but—"

"Lady Alice Hemsworth, before any further interruptions present themselves, will you do me the honor of promising to become my wife?"

"Yes." Her heart pounded. "Yes, yes, yes." She caught his face between her hands and kissed him. Deeply and passionately as love welled in her heart.

Herr Krause groaned. With a gasp, she pulled away. "We could celebrate, except—"

Ben caught her lips for another brief kiss. "We *will* celebrate. But later. Krause can't be found inside your compartment. Better if he's found trussed and unconscious within his own. We'll keep watch until we reach London. I've a feeling that presenting your prisoner to the Duke of Avesbury will do much to strengthen your consideration for an eventual position within the Queen's agents."

"I expect it will." She beamed, every fiber of her being

suffused with love. If only she could show him just how much. Alas, they had a body to drag down a corridor.

CHAPTER FIVE

Krause wasn't a large man. But—though Ben was rapidly recovering—whatever drug the German had loaded within the clockwork beetle's assassination needle, left him feeling as if he'd spent a week in bed subsisting on weak tea and broth. As such, he couldn't simply toss the man's limp form over his shoulder and haul him from carriage to carriage.

Though grateful Krause's villainy had brought them back together, his presence was now an obstacle for all the plans Ben had made for the compartment's mattress. Disappointing, but there would be time enough for that another day.

Rolling onto his stomach, he retrieved his pistol, then pushed to his feet and tucked the weapon into his waistband. Not a chance he'd give Krause another opportunity to do them harm.

Alice snatched up the key she'd pulled from Krause's

pocket. "His room key." Ben held out a hand and helped her to her feet. After shaking out her champagne-stained skirts, she lifted a hand to her hair. Half-pinned, half-loose, *all* of it was a mad tangle. Never had she looked so beautiful. He was utterly besotted. "Shall we?" she asked, hand on the door handle. "The train will soon reach Newcastle, where we're likely to draw an unwanted amount of attention."

"And further tarnish your reputation?" He let a corner of his mouth quirk upward. Life with Alice would be anything but dull.

"I do intend to restore it, beginning with an extravagant wedding with hundreds of guests. No one will wish to miss the event of the Season. Not only will that pacify my mother, it will give my father something to grumble about while he secretly rejoices that I will at last be safely wed. At the wedding breakfast, you will charm your way into the clubs and offices of the *ton*, and I will put on display my finest manners."

Ben barked a laugh. "All while wishing you could retire to your laboratory."

"Of course." She grinned. "But first, we have a would-be assassin to cage." She opened the door and stuck her head out. Her voice fell to a whisper. "All clear."

Towing the German by his collar, Ben followed her into the hallway, uncaring if the man acquired yet more scrapes and bruises. He deserved every last one. Already, Alice had tested the key in the adjoining compartment's door. She glanced at him and gave a quick shake of her head.

The key opened none of the compartments. There was

no choice but to cross into the next carriage or to drag the German back to Alice's compartment.

He'd heard rumor that an improved gangway was under design, one that would facilitate movement between carriages while the train was in motion, a feature desperately required were the swift steam trains to compete for customers with the slower, but more luxurious, dirigibles overhead. Unfortunately, such passages had yet to be installed.

"We should go back," he suggested. Caring a limp body across the gangway would be tricky. They might well drop Krause. Not that Ben would much mind if the villain were to fall beneath the iron wheels. It was Alice's safety that concerned him.

Lips pressed into a grim, determined line, Alice shook her head. "We can do this. Let me help."

Resigned, Ben opened the door. *Click, click. Click click.* Cinders stung the skin of his face, and cool night air rushed inward, whipping at Alice's hair and gown. Moonlight served as their only illumination.

"Careful," Ben said through gritted teeth. "Hold his ankles while I lift him over the coupling. Be careful not to catch your gown on the chains." Chains, though flexible, were a poor substitute for sturdy railings. "Drop him if you must."

"So noted." She bent to catch at Krause's ankles. "Swiftly, please," Alice said, her voice strained by the effort of lifting the man's dead weight.

Together, they lurched and pitched into the next

sleeping carriage. *Thunk.* Alice dropped Krause's feet and hurried forward, to try the key at the next door. No good. A second door.

Click. She glanced up, triumphant, and pushed the door inward.

"Halt!" a male voice called from within.

Ben dropped Krause's head—which made a satisfying *thud* upon the floor—and rushed to her rescue, hand upon his pistol. But it seemed the two were already acquainted, though the man made no move to lower the odd-looking weapon clutched in his fist.

"Mr. Jackson?" Alice gasped. "What are *you* doing on this train?"

A stunned silence followed. "I would ask the same of you." Mr. Jackson's eyes flicked to Ben. "I was informed Mr. Leighton was no longer... of interest. That you were... no longer in service."

Another Queen's agent.

"You were informed correctly," Alice replied, her voice haughty. "I do intend to remedy the second situation, a task with which Mr. Leighton is assisting me. Herr Krause attacked me in an attempt to secure a proprietary item that I am conveying to the Duke of Avesbury. We subdued him and thought to stash his unconscious form in his own compartment until the proper authorities could be contacted in London."

Slowly, Mr. Jackson lowered his weapon. "A happy coincidence, then. I was tasked with following the German myself, to determine his precise interests." He waved a hand at the numerous papers which were strewn across the bed. "Of which there are many. With such evidence, it is convenient that Herr Krause is bound and subdued. He's headed for a dank prison cell."

Ben sniffed an opportunity. "Coordinating your reports to the duke seems a wise approach," he suggested. "If Mr. Jackson is willing to detail your involvement in subduing Herr Krause, perhaps he might be permitted to take custody?" Thus freeing them from his care and allowing them to enjoy the remainder of the night.

Alice slid him a knowing look. "An acceptable compromise," she said. "I've an appointment with the duke tomorrow morning at eight. If you care to accompany me, you might make your report in person. I'm afraid, however, that you must then depart His Grace's office. The information I must pass to the duke is relevant to your case, but confidential."

It took great effort not to smile with admiration at Alice's coolheaded manipulation of the agent.

"Thank you, my lady." Relief washed over Mr. Jackson's face. "I would welcome the opportunity."

"Excellent." Ben dragged the German into his compartment and dropped him none too gently upon the floor. "He's begun to stir. You have sufficient restraints?"

Mr. Jackson nodded, then lifted his odd weapon. "Among other options. Rest assured, he will not escape."

As the door slammed closed behind them, Ben pulled a grinning Alice into his arms. "Nicely done. If the duke does not recognize what an asset you would be to the Queen's agents, then he's a fool."

She grinned. "We make a good team, you and I. Perhaps—"

He pressed a finger to her lips. "While I'm happy to assist you whenever necessary, I've no interest in becoming a spy, only in marrying one."

"Is that so?" She raised up on her toes and nibbled at his jaw, all the while unbuttoning his waistcoat. "Any interest in bedding one?"

No further invitation was necessary. With a low growl, Ben grabbed her by the hand and dragged her down the corridor.

WRAPPED in each other's arms, they tumbled through the doorway and fell against the wall. Pushing the tumbled tangle of hair from her face, Ben proceeded to kiss her senseless. Aether, he felt so right. Only an insistent and relentless dinging that she *knew* would not stop made her push him away.

"Watson," she gasped, waving.

Forgotten in the scuffle, Watson still hid underneath the bed. He'd ventured forth to stare up at them with gleaming green eyes above vibrating wire whiskers.

"The zoetomatic objects to our activities?" He nipped at her neck. "That's a problematic feature that must be adjusted."

"He *is* rather protective. Let me turn him off."

Ben stepped back and cocked his head. "On the contrary." He shrugged his waistcoat from his shoulders and tossed it aside. "Finish showing me his many features and tricks, so that I might fully appreciate the alluring mind of the woman who has finally agreed to marry me."

A faint blush crept onto her cheeks. Not at the flattery, but because—while he spoke—his fingers were deftly unbuttoning his shirt, revealing muscles she'd only before felt. The room in which she'd first given herself to him had been—regrettably—rather dark. Her mouth went dry. "A lecture? You expect coherent speech from me while you—"

His shirt fell open. A knowing grin curved his lips. "Be brief."

"He follows commands programmed into a cipher cartridge: model B257." She forced the words from her lips, not once looking at the zoetomatic. "And performs a few parlor tricks." She swallowed, tore her gaze away and issued a series of commands. "Watson. Spin." Watson spun in a circle. "Watson. Sit." He sat. "Watson. Beg." The metallic hedgehog straightened, balancing on his hind legs, front paws curled to his chest.

"Adorable," Ben said drily. His shirt landed atop the compartment's chair, and she had to remind herself to breathe. "But I've not yet seen anything that warrants sending an attack, clockwork beetle after you."

"Ah," she said, holding perfectly still as Ben's deft fingers turned their attention to the lacings that ran down her back.

"Let me show you." Her bodice fell loose and slid free. He was wasting no time. "Or it could wait."

"No," he whispered in her ear. "Don't stop."

The tapes and buttons and hooks would take him a few more minutes, and she did wish to show him the hedgehog's most technologically advanced elements. "Watson. Come."

The metallic hedgehog waddled across the floor to bump against her stocking-clad ankle, and she bent—interrupting Ben's attentions—to scoop it from the floor. "Watson. Prepare and assess." A number of the hedgehog's spines retracted and a multitude of oddly formed wire antennae extended to take their place.

"These probes..." Ben lifted an eyebrow. His fingers tugged and pulled at her gown.

"Analyze a variety of airborne chemical components. Twenty-two separate molecules." A faint whirring emanated from Watson as a variety of gears within turned, sampling the environment. "An alarm sounds if there's any threat to his handler. Or—if all is safe—Watson will whistle."

Ben's fingers stilled. "All within this tiny creature?" Doubt mixed with awe. His fingers flicked, and her skirts fell free. "That explains his insistent ringing when he detected the beetle climbing on your skirts."

"If only I'd activated him sooner." Alice twisted in his arms, holding Watson between them. "Miniaturization is my goal. A societal liaison ought to be able to carry about a personal zoetomatic without suspicion that it is anything other than a silly toy." She paused. "After our attack, I'm hoping to install a small rod that might shock an attacker.

There's not enough power to fully disable a man, but it might be enough of a distraction to allow its handler a chance to escape."

"You've been in such a situation?" Anger flared in his eyes.

"Once or twice." She did not wish to speak of it. Not at this particular moment. Another time. "Nothing I couldn't handle."

Ben frowned, but he let the topic slide when Watson emitted a clear, high-pitched sound. A whistle.

"All clear." She grinned proudly.

Ben tipped his head. "With all the internal mechanics necessary to perform these many tasks, what powers all this activity? For you've fed it not so much as a single lump of coal."

"Ah, and therein lies Herr Krause's interest." She tapped out a code on the zoetomatic's spines and the curved, inter-locking sections of its back retracted to reveal a hollow interior.

"And a concealed compartment," Ben said. "Most impressive." He lifted Watson from her hands and moved away to hold the zoetomatic closer to the Lucifer lamp bolted to the wall. He peered inside. "Is that... No." His head snapped up.

"It is." Warm satisfaction spread through her. "They said it could not be done."

"Yet you've managed it. A miniaturized Markoid battery. Most impressive. Is that what Krause wanted so very badly?"

"Along with the chemical analytic devices? Yes. The battery has its faults, and I'm afraid I've reached a bit of an impasse. I require a more in-depth understanding of cutting-edge mechanical engineering theory. Not to mention colleagues. I tried to speak with Professor Armstrong at the University of Edinburgh, but was turned away."

"Ah, that explains your unaccompanied excursion." Ben leaned closer. "How on earth did you escape to Scotland unaccompanied?"

A sly smile stretched her lips. "My Aunt Ellie makes a wonderful co-conspirator. But even she can't suppress *all* the London gossips."

Ben grinned in response. "I'm looking forward to meeting this relative of yours. At the very least, I'll ensure she is seated in the front row at our wedding." He twitched one of Watson's spines, and the hedgehog curled once more into a silver ball. "Did she not know of the German man who paid you far too much attention?"

A topic she and her aunt had discussed at length. "Neither of us thought Herr Krause would follow me all the way to Scotland, but this past month, he has dogged my steps, pressing me to discuss my work."

"Is there any chance he knew of your connection to the Queen's agents? Of your wish to attend the Rankine institute?"

"I can't see how he possibly could, unless there's a leak within the organization?" She paused, thinking. "But shortly after I presented the duke with my plans, Herr Krause became rather insistent, going so far as to make me a generous offer for the device, sight unseen."

"I can imagine." He set Watson carefully aside and—hooking a finger over the edge of her corset—drew her close. A shudder of desire rushed through her. Their hips bumped, and she leaned into him, enjoying the crush of her breast against his chest and the gentle friction of her hips against his. All this technical talk had not dimmed his other interest at all. "To think of the number of devices it might power..."

Alice smoothed her hands over the hard planes of his chest. "Only small ones." She pressed a kiss to the hollow of his throat, grinning when a soft moan escaped his mouth. "And only for a short period of time." She slid her arms about his neck. "There's not enough stored chemical energy to power a full-sized steambot for more than a few minutes."

"My mind has begun to stumble." He ran the tip of his finger over the swell of her breasts, then toyed with the topmost fastening of her corset. "Perhaps we might table technological discussions for an hour or two? I'm of a mind to turn my attention to research of another kind."

"My thoughts exactly." And with that, she drew his lips to hers and immersed herself in the many sensations of her newest—and most favorite—past time.

EPILOGUE

Alice—flanked by both Ben and Mr. Jackson —
followed the duke's antiquated steam butler,
Burton, wondering why no one bothered to oil
his rusty jaw. But it was not her place to inquire. She rubbed
her finger over the drawstring of her reticule in nervous
excitement, then forced herself to stop. Only the most
proper behavior must be on display this morning. And that
included suppressing the overwhelming desire to smile at
the loyal—if exhausted—man who had accompanied her
from the train station directly to the duke's doorstep.

Upon their arrival at King's Cross, Clara had clapped
her hands. "Thank goodness," she'd whispered in Alice's ear.
"I was afraid I might find myself related to Lady Delphinia.
Alas, it's far too early an hour to properly celebrate. We'll
have tea soon." Grinning, Ben's sister had adjusted her hat,
then climbed into a separate steam carriage.

Alice and Ben had been celebrating their engagement all

night, but she was anything but tired. Pure excitement and anticipation galvanized her.

Her mouth twitched. Affianced to the very man the duchess had instructed her to abandon, their next stop would be her parent's London townhome, where Mother would be promised anything she wanted, provided it hastened their wedding without attracting negative speculations as to the reason why.

All that remained was to secure herself a position of favor with Her Grace's husband, the Duke of Avesbury.

Burton rolled to a stop before the great man's door, and Alice's stomach flip-flopped. Unclenching her fingers, she smoothed her skirts. She'd chosen a modest, russet-striped day gown with a high necked and pleated bodice—edged by two simple rows of buttons—and an overskirt that swept back into a high bustle to highlight the triangular-toothed russet accents of her skirts. All very tasteful. A shame her oversized reticule did not precisely match. If Her Grace was present, she would note the faux pas. Alice was counting on Watson's brilliance—and the captured clockwork insect—to distract the duke from any disapproval his duchess might insinuate.

Ben gave her hand a furtive squeeze and whispered, "Good luck!" Then took a step back, prepared to wait as long as necessary while she met with the duke.

"My lady." Burton waved her into the study.

Alice lifted her chin and preceded Mr. Jackson into a wood-paneled room lined with shelves of books. Traditional gas jets helped the windows to illuminate the room. The great man himself stood behind a large, wooden desk. Alas, Her Grace did indeed sit in a wing-backed chair beside the fireplace. She did not look up from her needlework.

Alice swallowed and tamped down her concern. "Thank you for agreeing to meet with me, Your Grace."

"Lady Alice," the duke replied, inclining his head. "And Mr. Jackson. To what do I owe this additional pleasure?"

"A would-be thief provided us both some... difficulties last night," she began. "Mr. Jackson was good enough to help detain him so that your agents might question him." She took a deep breath. "Perhaps he might provide his report first? The device which I hope to demonstrate is, as you know, of a rather sensitive nature."

The duchess sniffed, but set aside her stitching—was that a needlepoint likeness of the Queen's face?—to turn her disapproving gaze upon them. "Is that wise, my dear, allowing a dismissed liaison to stand witness to an agent's report?"

"Perhaps." The duke tipped his head, considering his wife's words.

Mr. Jackson cleared his throat. "Your Grace, the papers confiscated from Herr Krause's compartment are coded and will require extensive analysis. At this time, I've only been able to decipher a small portion of their content. My presence here is only to inform you that the German is safely in custody for which we have Lady Alice and Mr. Leighton to thank."

"Mr. Benjamin Leighton?" The duchess's eyebrows rose. "Is that so?"

Alice flushed. "It is."

"If that's all?" the duke asked his agent.

"It is, Your Grace."

"If I may?" Alice interrupted. "Mr. Jackson is unaware that Herr Krause sent a clockwork beetle, intended for me, fitted with a spring-released hypodermic needle into my compartment. While I was targeted, Mr. Leighton was the unfortunate recipient of a hefty dose of an unknown toxin." She reached into her reticule and pulled forth her jar of face cream. "It has been temporarily immobilized, but I would advise it undergo further study."

Both men's eyes grew wide.

"See it done, Mr. Jackson," the duke commanded. "Dismissed."

With a formal bow, Mr. Jackson departed, canister in hand.

"Due to pressing concerns this morning, our time is limited, Lady Alice," the duke prompted. "Your letter indicated you managed to construct the contraption we discussed, one that might be of extraordinary use to the Queen's agents and societal liaisons?"

"I have, Your Grace." Quickly, Alice pulled the deceptively simple silver ball from her reticule. "With the twitch of his activation spine..."

Alice ran through Watson's many features and talents.

Within seconds, she had the duke's rapt attention.

And the duchess's grudging admiration. "Perhaps I was a bit precipitate in dismissing your value as a societal liaison. If I were to reinstate you, would you be willing?"

The duke snorted. *Snorted!* "I doubt it, my dear. Mr. Leighton is standing in our hall as we speak. This can only mean one thing."

The duchess twisted her lips. "Invite him in, Lady Alice."

Stomach churning, Alice pulled open the duke's door and waved a hand at Ben. "Come," she hissed, "they wish to speak to *you*."

"Me?"

"Behave," Alice warned.

"Of course." He followed her into the study, then bowed in greeting. "Your Graces."

"Mr. Leighton," the duchess began. "Am I to understand you have proposed to this young lady?"

"I have."

"And she has accepted?"

Ben's eyes glinted. "Enthusiastically."

The duchess narrowed her eyes. "Hrmph."

"You are aware, then," the duke said. "Of her career aspirations, ones that will call her away from household management?"

"I am," Ben answered. "I'm fully prepared to support her goals in any way possible."

Alice beamed as her chest filled with love and pride.

"Well, then," the duke smiled. "May I be the first to wish you happy. Be certain to send us an invitation."

Ben shot Alice a speaking glance. The attendance of the duke and duchess at their wedding would not only quell any rumors about their time together on the train, it would open doors that would otherwise have remained tightly closed.

"We will, Your Grace."

The duke cleared his throat. "On the topic of zoetomatics, once you've had the opportunity to speak with engineers already in our employ, I'd like to arrange for a trial with an active societal liaison." The duke shared a look with his duchess. "I have just the young lady in mind."

Her Grace let out a protracted sigh. "Very well. She might trial it, but only because she has been steadfastly dedicated to her mission."

"Congratulations, Lady Alice," the duke said. "I'll instruct the admissions department of the Rankine Institute to contact you. Once you have a handle on your coursework, we will discuss further employment opportunities."

Ben managed to wait until the study door closed behind them—but barely—before he swept Alice off her feet, swinging her about with a triumphant cry of glee. "You did it!"

Billows of disapproving steam emerged from beneath the steam butler's collar as he flapped his jointed hands, uncertain how to chase such poorly behaved guests from the house.

Laughing as her heart swelled near to bursting, Alice gave him a quick kiss. "Now put me down before anyone catches us." He obliged. "You've my mother to pacify. Step quickly, we must reach her before the rumors."

ABOUT THE AUTHOR

Though ANNE RENWICK holds a Ph.D. in biology and greatly enjoyed tormenting the overburdened undergraduates who were her students, fiction has always been her first love. Today, she writes steampunk romance, placing a new kind of biotech in the hands of mad scientists, proper young ladies and determined villains.

Anne brings an unusual perspective to steampunk. A number of years spent locked inside the bowels of a biological research facility left her permanently altered. In her steampunk world, the Victorian fascination with all things anatomical led to a number of alarming biotechnological advances. Ones that the enemies of Britain would dearly love to possess.

www.AnneRenwick.com

instagram.com/anne_renwick
facebook.com/AnneRenwickAuthor
pinterest.com/AuthorAnneRenwick

www.ingramcontent.com/pod-product-compliance
Lightning Source LLC
Chambersburg PA
CBHW032043180726
48284CB00008B/2724